Jake, Ace Detective

Written by Margaret Ryan
Illustrated by Amanda Wood

Chapter 1

No school today, YIPPEE! All the teachers are at school, but all the children have the day off – great! I can help Mum at the surgery.

Mum's a vet. I might be a vet too, when I grow up – AFTER I've been a world class footballer, of course!

'Hurry up, Jake, and put Winston into the car. We'll be late for the surgery,' called Jake's mum.

That's my mum. She's got wild hair and a 'Save the Tiger' T-shirt. Winston is my dog. He's a Great Dane. He's a great dog.

Winston jumped into the back of the car and began to snore. He's a brilliant snorer. I got in beside Mum. She doesn't snore – not when she's driving down country roads, anyway.

When we got to the surgery it was full of people and pets.

'It looks like we're going to be busy today,' said Mum.

Just then, Julie, the nurse, came over with a cardboard box.

'What's in there?' I asked.

'Have a look,' said Julie.

Inside the box was a stripy kitten.

'I found him on the doorstep,' said Julie. 'I wonder who left him there?'

Mum shook her head. 'It was
probably someone who couldn't
look after him. We must find him
a good home, but I'm too busy
right now.'

'I'll look after the kitten,' I said.

I took the box from Julie and went outside to show Winston. I carefully put the box down on the ground and Winston pushed his head right inside the box. He is so nosey! He made a little squeaky noise when he saw the kitten.

The kitten looked up and squeaked back.

Then I had a brilliant idea. I
ran back to tell Julie my plan.
'But keep it a secret from Mum,'
I said.

'Okay,' grinned Julie.

While Mum was busy looking
at a rabbit's sore ear, I picked up
the box with the kitten.

'Come on, little fellow,' I said. 'I
know where I can find you a
good home.'

Winston and I left the surgery and walked along the village street. Everyone stopped to chat to Winston and to offer him sweets. Winston loves sweets.

Hello, Winston!

Give me a paw, Winston.

Would you like a sweet, Winston?

At last we came to the corner shop. Mrs Franks, the shopkeeper, was putting tins on a shelf.

'Hello, Jake. Hello, Winston,' she said.

'Hello, Mrs Franks. I've brought something for you.' I opened up the box.

'Ooh!' said Mrs Franks. 'What a lovely kitten.'

Jake said, 'Someone left him on our doorstep at the surgery. We don't know who. He needs a good home and I know you had a mouse in the shop yesterday. . .'

'How clever you are, Jake,' said Mrs Franks. I was thinking about getting a cat. Here's some chocolate for you and Winston for being so kind.'

'Thank you,' I said.

'Woof! woof!' Winston barked.

Winston loves chocolate.

I munched all the way back to the surgery. So did Winston.

We were just finishing the last bit of chocolate, when we nearly tripped over something on the surgery doorstep. It was another cardboard box. Guess what was inside? Another stripy kitten.

Chapter 2

'Who could have left another stripy kitten?' I said.

Winston shook his head.

'I'm going to find out,' I said. 'I'm going to be Jake, Ace Detective!'

I went to tell Mum about kitten number two, but she was still busy mending a dog's broken leg. I knew where I could find another good home, so I called out to Julie, 'We're just going to see our friends at York House.'

York House is where the old folk live. Winston and I often go up there to visit.

We left the surgery, crossed at the zebra crossing, and walked up the hill. Everyone stopped to chat to Winston and to offer him doggy chocs. Winston loves doggy chocs.

Good boy, Winston.

Give me a paw, Winston.

Hello, Winston. Would you like some doggy chocs?

At last we came to the old folk's house. It was a sunny morning and all the old folk were sitting in the garden.

'Hello, Jake. Hello, Winston,' they said. 'It's nice to see you. We're just going to have our morning coffee. Would you like some biscuits?'

I nodded. So did Winston. Winston loves biscuits.

'I've brought someone else to see you this morning,' I said. I opened up the cardboard box.

'Ooh, it's a kitten. Isn't she lovely?' they all said.

Sister Davis came out of the big house to see what all the fuss was about. Winston charged over to her.

He tucked his nose in her pocket. That's where she usually keeps his custard creams. Winston loves custard creams.

'Hello, Sister Davis,' I said. 'I've brought a kitten for York House. Someone left her on our doorstep at the surgery. We don't know who, though I'm trying to find out. We need a good home for her, and I know how much all of you love animals.'

Sister Davis smiled. 'She is lovely, Jake, and everyone would enjoy making a fuss of her. So. . .yes, of course we'd love to have her.'

'Hooray!' shouted everyone.
'What shall we call her?' asked
one lady.

I grinned and left before war
broke out, and before the old
folk found out that Winston had
eaten all their custard creams.

We shared mine on the way home, and I kept wondering who could have left the kittens on our doorstep. It couldn't be the mother cat herself because both of the kittens had arrived in cardboard boxes. So it had to be a person. But who?

'Being an ace detective isn't as easy as I thought!' I said to Winston.

Then, when we got back to the surgery, we nearly tripped over something on the doorstep. It was another cardboard box. And guess what was inside? Another stripy kitten!

Chapter 3

I went to tell Mum about kitten number three, but she was busier than ever. Mrs Robb's cat had eaten a baby's dummy. That cat will eat anything. He's nearly as bad as Winston.

'We're just going to see Kate and Mark,' I called to Julie. Winston and I set off.

Kate and Mark are twins. They're in my class at school. It's their birthday next week, and they're having a fancy dress party. I'm going as a footballer. Mum wants to buy Kate and Mark books and a video, but I've had a much better idea.

When I arrived, Kate and Mark were supposed to be washing their dad's car. Instead, they were throwing water at each other.

Sploosh! Splish! Splash! Splosh!

'GOT YOU!' yelled Kate.

'THAT'S NOT FAIR! I WASN'T READY!' called Mark.

'Hi, Jake. Hi, Winston,' said Kate. 'Do you want a water fight?'

'Later,' I said. 'Look, I've brought you something.' I opened up the cardboard box.

'Ooh, a kitten,' said Mark. 'He's lovely.'

'Someone left him on our doorstep at the surgery. We don't know who, though I'm trying to find out. He needs a good home, and I know it's your birthday next week. . .'

At that moment, Kate and Mark's dad, Mr Peel, came out to see if his car was clean yet.

'Can we have a kitten for our birthday , Dad? Pleeeeeaase,' said Kate and Mark. 'This one needs a good home, and we love him already.'

'But will you look after him properly?' asked their dad. 'You need to give him food and water. He needs a basket to sleep in and some toys to play with. You can't just put him away, like an old teddy bear, when you're fed up with him.'

'That's what my mum says,' I nodded.

Kate and Mark promised to take good care of the kitten.

We went inside and played with the kitten for ages. When he fell asleep, we went outside and had our water fight. It was brilliant. I got really wet.

Winston stayed inside with Mr Peel. He gave Winston a carrot to crunch. Winston loves carrots.

Then it was time to go back to the surgery.

'I don't think I make a very good Ace Detective,' I said to Winston, as we walked along the village street. 'I haven't managed to find out who was leaving all those kittens.'

When we got back to the surgery, Mrs Price and her cat, Tigger, were in the waiting room. Tigger used to be fat, but now she was quite thin.

Suddenly, something in my brain went *PING!* Suddenly, I knew who was leaving the kittens. Suddenly, I WAS an ace detective!

'I see Tigger's had her kittens, Mrs Price,' I said.

'Yes, six weeks ago, Jake,' said Mrs Price. 'She's had three.'

'Have you been leaving Tigger's kittens for us?' I asked.

'Yes,' said Mrs Price. 'I can't manage to look after them any more, and I knew your mum would find them good homes.'

I grinned. Mrs Price didn't know it yet, but I had solved THAT problem.

'I couldn't carry the kittens all at once, so I brought them one at a time,' went on Mrs Price. 'I wanted to speak to your mum about them, but she was always so busy.'

'But not quite so busy now,' said Mum, coming into the waiting room. She was still wearing her 'Save the Tiger' T-shirt, but now she had a budgie on her head. It probably thought her wild hair was a nest!

'So it was Tigger's kitten, was it, Mrs Price?' asked Mum. 'I should have guessed. As soon as I've finished here, I'll see if I can find a good home for him.'

'No need,' I grinned. 'I've done that already. AND for kitten number two! AND for kitten number three!'

I told them all about Mrs Franks, the old folk and Kate and Mark.

Mrs Price was delighted. So was my mum.

'Well done, Jake,' she said. 'As a treat, how would you like to have a cheeseburger and chips for lunch?'

'Great!' I said. 'Ace detectives love cheeseburgers and chips!'

WOOF! WOOF!

And so does Winston!